W9-BBA-538

POWER FAILURE

Written by Mary O'Neill
Illustrated and Designed by John Bindon

Library of Congress Cataloging-in-Publication Data

O'Neill, Mary, (date)
  Power failure / by Mary O'Neill; illustrated by John Bindon.
    p.   cm.—(SOS planet earth)
  Summary: Discusses the energy sources we use today and those that
might power the world of the future.
  ISBN 0-8167-2288-9 (lib. bdg.)   ISBN 0-8167-2289-7 (pbk.)
  1. Power resources—Juvenile literature.   2. Renewable energy
sources—Juvenile literature.   3. Energy conservation—Juvenile
literature.   [1. Power resources.]   I. Bindon, John, ill.
II. Title.   III. Series.
TH163.23.O54   1991
333.79—dc20   90-11148

Published by Troll Associates, Mahwah, New Jersey in
association with Vanwell Publishing Limited.
Printed in the United States of America.

10   9   8   7   6   5   4   3   2   1

Troll Associates

About This Book...

We live in a world full of energy! All around us, tools that use energy help us go places and do things that have never been possible before. But energy use has a price. Our machines, tools, and toys get their energy from fuel that cannot easily be replaced or reused.

Energy use causes some of our biggest problems today. For example, we are slowly running out of some of our most important fuels, like oil and coal. It will take many years before we have found ways to replace these fuels. In the future, we could face fuel shortages that stop us in our tracks.

We face an even greater problem right now. Many of the fuels we use create pollution that is choking our world. If we want to have clean air, water, and soil for tomorrow, we have to find cleaner fuels today.

In this book you will learn about the energy we depend on and how it affects our planet. You will also read about the kinds of energy that might power the world of the future. We all have to do our part to make the earth a clean-energy world. Captain Conservation will give you some ideas on how you can get started right away.

Read on, and find out more about energy...

Contents

Energy—The Get Up and Go

What do a moving car, a growing plant, and a human body all have in common? They all need some form of energy to move and grow. Energy is what puts things into action. In fact, the word "energy" comes from the Greek word *energeia*, which means "active."

You might know that oil, gas, coal, and electricity are all sources of energy. But most people don't realize that energy is everywhere around us. Sun, wind, steam, and moving water are also sources of energy. And so are atoms, the tiny particles that make up all matter in the universe. In fact, everything that moves has energy.

Fuel for Our Bodies

Just like cars, we humans have to fill up with fuel to keep going. The food we eat is the fuel that supplies us with energy. This energy produces body heat that keeps our body's basic activities—such as breathing and heartbeat—going. It also gives our muscles the power for lifting, running, and jumping.

Our bodies store the energy we get from food as a sugar called glucose. When energy is needed, the glucose is broken down. This releases the stored energy along with a little water and a gas called carbon dioxide.

As glucose breaks down, it releases energy to strengthen muscles.

Plants—The Power to Make Food

Much of our food comes from the plants we eat. But where do plants get the energy to make this food? They get their energy from the sun in the form of light energy. Plants use this energy to take in carbon dioxide from the air and mix it with water and nutrients from the soil. Some of this energy is used to keep the plant alive. The leftover energy is stored in the leaves, roots, and other parts of the plant.

Making Things Work for Us

Humans have invented many machines to do work for us. Machines take us places, keep our homes warm, provide light, or make different objects for us to use. All of these machines need a source of energy.

People have learned to take energy from many different sources. You don't have to look far to find energy in action. The light you read by is probably powered by electricity. Your home might be heated by natural gas, coal, oil, or electricity. If your family has a car, it most likely runs on gasoline. In school you might find calculators powered by the sun. And power tools work only when they have a source of energy.

Absorbs
carbon dioxide
(CO_2)

Releases Oxygen
(O_2)

Glucose
is stored
in potatoes
($C_6 H_{12} O_6 + 6O_2$)

Absorbs
water
(H_2O)

Captain Conservation:
Go on an Energy Safari!

You can probably "hunt" down many types of energy in your own home. See if you can find things that run on these different fuels: coal, oil, gas, electricity, and solar power (the power of the sun). Which of these things are used most often in your home? Do you turn them on only when needed?

Earth's Energy Systems

Planet Earth is a natural storehouse of power. Nearly all of earth's energy starts with the sun. Without the sun's heat, this would be a lifeless and frozen planet. But the sun does more than keep us warm and make plants grow. It prevents much of the earth's water from freezing. This makes rivers flow and water in lakes and oceans move. The sun's heat also changes water into vapor to form clouds and makes the air surrounding the earth move to produce wind.

The moon is another natural source of energy. It causes the back-and-forth movement of the oceans that we call tides.

The earth's natural energy systems of sun, wind, and tides can be harnessed to do work for us. These sources of energy can never be used up. We call these limitless sources of power "renewable energy."

Not to scale

The Hard-Working Sun

The sun is more than 90 million miles (150 million kilometers) from the earth. Yet even from this great distance it provides our planet with enough heat and light to make life possible. Because we are so far away, we receive only a tiny fraction of all the energy released by the sun. But even this amount is equal to the energy produced by nearly 200 million power stations!

Not all of the sun's energy can be used directly by humans. About one third is reflected by the earth's surface back into space.[1] Close to half is used by the earth's atmosphere to keep air, water, and land warm.[2] And nearly one quarter of the sun's heat is used to make water evaporate[3] (change into gas). A tiny portion of the sun's energy, less than one percent, creates our winds and air currents. And even less energy than this provides the light used by all growing plants.

6

Capturing the Wind

If you have ever been in a sailboat, you know the kind of work wind can do. Wind can be used to move things directly. For many centuries people have used windmills to grind grain. Today wind is also used to make electricity.

Water Power

River water can move very quickly. The force of this rushing water can be a great source of power. People in some areas still use the power of water to do work directly. For example, water-driven mills can grind wheat into flour. But most water power today produces electricity.

Energy From the Ocean

Oceans cover more than two thirds of the world's surface. This water stores a vast amount of energy. Much of this energy cannot be used yet. But new technology could turn the ocean into a future source of power. Someday we may be able to use the warmth of tropical ocean water to make electricity. Projects in some areas are already capturing the energy of tides. The back-and-forth motion of the ocean water is used to make electricity.

Power Within the Earth

The earth itself is a source of heat energy. At the center of our planet lies a hot core. This heat from the earth's center warms water trapped below the surface. In many parts of the world, springs of hot water escape upward through the surface. These springs are called hot geysers. Steam produced by hot geysers can be used to make electricity. In the future, we may be able to use the heat below our planet's surface in many other ways.

Earth's Hidden Stores of Energy

The sun is also the indirect source of the energy buried beneath the earth's surface in the form of coal, oil, and gas. We call these buried treasures fossil fuels. Like fossils, these fuels formed from plants and animals that lived long ago. Unlike renewable energy, fossil fuels will not last forever. Once they are used up, they cannot be replaced. It would take many millions of years for the earth to rebuild its store of fossil fuels.

Fuels From Ancient Life

With the help of sunlight, living plants combine carbon dioxide from the air with water from the soil. From these ingredients plants make food that contains carbon and hydrogen. This food is taken in by animals when they eat the plants. The energy is then stored in their bodies. When plants and animals die, the stored energy in their bodies does not just disappear. Over many millions of years, it may change into the different forms that we call fossil fuels. Although coal, oil, and gas all look quite different, they are all formed from the carbon and hydrogen once trapped in the bodies of plants and animals.

Coal

The coal we now burn as fuel began forming even before dinosaurs walked the earth. Two hundred and fifty million years ago, lush plant life covered the planet. New layers of plants quickly replaced those that died before them. Normally oxygen in the soil helps break down the dead plants. This releases their stored energy as heat. But during periods of heavy rain, some of the dead matter was trapped in the wet soil. As the wet soil held little oxygen, the dead matter couldn't break down. Over millions of years, new layers of earth built up. The weight of this earth squeezed the plant matter into a layer called peat. In many countries today peat is cut, dried, and burned for heat. But it is also a middle stage in the formation of coal. As more land built up over the peat, it was packed more tightly into coal.

Carboniferous swamp

Coal

Oil

Oil is an older cousin of coal. It also formed from dead matter long buried beneath the earth. But it takes much longer for oil to form. Oil began with tiny plants and animals that lived in the sea four to five hundred million years ago. As they died, their bodies sank to the ocean floor, building up a store of carbon and hydrogen. As layers of this dead matter built up, the heat and pressure of the earth changed the carbon and hydrogen first into rock and finally into oil.

Oil is found below the earth, trapped in rock. Oil doesn't just fill a huge hole between solid layers of rock. It is found mixed in a special type of rock made up of tiny grains with spaces between them. The liquid oil fills these spaces. Because it flows easily, the oil is pushed upward by the heat of the earth. It rises until it meets a layer of hard rock it can't pass through. When trapped there, the oil forms a huge underground pool that we call an oil field.

Natural Gas

Heat and lack of oxygen underneath the earth's surface make our planet a natural gas maker. Because gas is light in weight, it rises toward the surface. Like oil, it becomes trapped beneath layers of hard rock where it collects and forms fields of gas. Later the gas can be reached and taken out by drilling through the rock.

Since gas is lighter than oil, a layer of gas often forms above an oil field. In the past, oil companies simply burned off the gas that rose from the ground as they drilled for oil. But today the gas is saved and used as a valuable fuel, too.

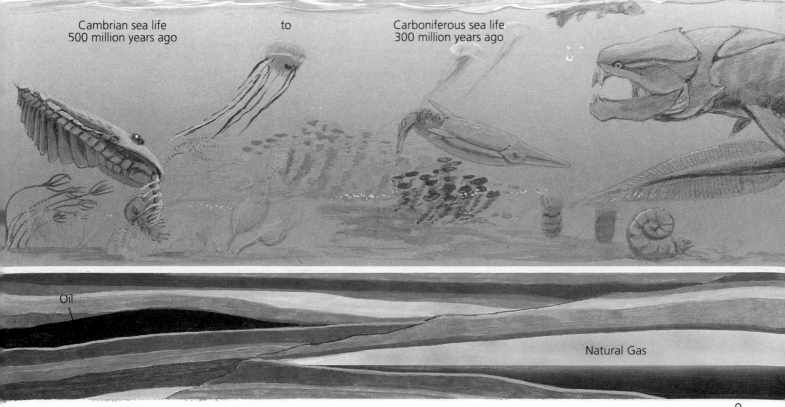

Cambrian sea life
500 million years ago

to

Carboniferous sea life
300 million years ago

Oil

Natural Gas

Powering a World of Industry

One of the things that makes humans different from other animals is our special talent for invention. We can make comfortable homes in harsh places. We've invented machines that can take us long distances. Our special way of life is possible because we can make many different types of energy do work for us.

Harnessing Nature

The first humanlike creatures appeared about four million years ago. Like other animals, they probably warmed themselves in the sun and got their energy from the foods they ate. Later our ancestors began to use fire. Perhaps they first used fire that started in the wild when lightning struck a tree. They might then have "captured" this fire to keep their campfires burning for warmth, light, and protection against wild animals. Humans first learned how to start their own fires about 700 thousand years ago. This discovery greatly changed people's lives. The ability to create heat allowed people to stay in the same area when the weather turned cold in winter. They could travel to new areas that had been too cold to live in before.

As people settled, they began to plant crops for food. Farming brought many new inventions. The plow used the energy of animals to turn the soil. The energy of wind and moving water was captured by mills to grind wheat and draw water.

As farming spread, towns sprang up around the earth. People looked for new ways to travel and to bring their goods to other places to trade. For thousands of years, the quickest way to get around was to use the strength of animals. Hitched to wagons, chariots, or sleds, animals could also pull heavy loads. In North America horses and mules pulled wagons and carriages or carried people on their backs. Camels carried people and huge packs across the deserts of North Africa. And in Asia people rode on elephants and used them to haul heavy loads.

Compared to the cars, jets, and trains of today, these animals moved slowly. Their slow pace kept people from traveling quickly into new areas. All of this changed with a new invention—the steam engine.

The Power of Steam

If you've ever noticed the lid of a boiling pot rattle, you've seen steam at work. As liquid changes to gas, it takes up more space. The expanding gas puts pressure on whatever stands in its way. This pressure causes the object to move. The steam engine harnessed the energy of moving gas molecules. It put this energy to work to turn the wheels on trains or the paddles on steamships.

With the invention of the steam engine, travel really took off! And so did industry. The steam engine could be used in all kinds of machines. It speeded up the spinning of cotton and improved water pumps for underground mines. People no longer had to depend on the strength of animals or the power of wind and water to do work. Now people could make machines work by the power of steam wherever and whenever they were needed.

Steam

A slide valve directs steam to force a piston to move up and down.

Slide valve

Piston

Water

Air

A spark ignites the vapor forcing the piston to move up and down.

Carburetor

Gas mixes with air to produce an explosive vapor.

Of course, people needed some form of energy to make the steam. Early engines had separate boiler tanks where coal was burned to heat water. As steam-driven machines spread across Europe and North America in the late 1800s, coal became the most important source of fuel.

Making the Wheels Spin Faster

The steam engine made long-distance travel by train and ship much quicker. But many people continued to use animals for their everyday travels. Steam engines were large and heavy. They were not well suited to vehicles that carried small numbers of people.

A new invention in the late 1800s burned fuel in an engine instead of in a separate boiler. This meant the engines could be made much smaller. And since the new engines burned fuel inside, or internally, they were called internal-combustion engines.

Internal-combustion engines couldn't run on coal. They needed a liquid fuel that could be burned right inside. Gasoline, a product made from oil, quickly became the favorite fuel for cars. It was a light liquid that contained a great deal of energy. As new ways to process oil into gasoline were invented, driving became much cheaper. More people bought cars. With all of these cars taking to the road, the demand for gasoline rose quickly. Oil became the main energy source of the twentieth century.

A Bright Idea

Turning on a light wasn't always as easy as flicking a switch. Thomas Edison invented the light bulb in 1879. Before then, people burned whale oil or kerosene (an oil product) in lamps. The new electric lights were so popular that in just a few years whole cities were lit by these glowing bulbs.

11

Tough Energy Choices

Today our lives depend on machines that gobble energy. But there is a limit to many important energy supplies. Fossil fuels such as coal, oil, and gas are running out. And renewable energy sources such as solar power, wind, and tidal power don't yet meet all our needs.

We're also learning that the ways we use energy can do great damage to our planet. Pollution caused by using certain fuels may make life more difficult for all who share the earth. Because of the pollution caused by some forms of energy and the shortages we will face in the future, we have some tough energy choices to make.

The Energy We Use Today

Oil is our main source of energy today. It supplies over a third of all our energy. The fossil fuels—coal, oil, and gas combined—make up more than three quarters of all the energy we use.

The next largest source of energy is called biomass. Biomass is plant or animal matter that can be burned as fuel. Most biomass energy comes from firewood. This is the largest source of energy in the developing world. In countries with few industries, most energy is used in simple wood fires mainly for cooking.

We have barely begun to tap the renewable energy around us. Falling water used as hydropower is the most developed form of renewable energy. Yet it makes up only five percent of our energy supply. We are only beginning to explore the power of the sun, wind, oceans, and the earth's warm depths.

Nuclear power is a new type of energy that has only been in use for a few decades. Today it provides about four percent of the energy we use. Nuclear energy may offer an endless supply of electricity. But it also produces deadly wastes that must be carefully stored for thousands of years. Many people feel that these wastes and the chance of accidents make nuclear power too dangerous.

Time Is Running Out

As each year passes, we use up more and more fuel that cannot be replaced. Oil is likely to disappear first. Using oil as fast as we do today, we will probably run out of our supply sometime between the beginning and middle of the twenty-first century. Coal will probably be the longest lasting fossil fuel. Yet even it will only last about another two hundred years.

People living in developing countries are already short of firewood, their main energy source. Two billion people depend on firewood for energy. Most of them must go without fuel from time to time. The growing search for wood also means that forests in these areas are often·stripped bare.

A Hot, Hazy Future?

Even if we were not running short of fossil fuels, we would still have to look for other forms of energy. Burning fossil fuels creates pollution. The three main problems we face from continued use of fossil fuels are smog, acid rain, and the greenhouse effect.

Smog

In crowded cities pollution from burning coal, oil, and gas creates a poisonous haze called smog. Some of the gases and particles in these fumes can cause breathing and skin problems. Even mild smog can give you a sore throat, aching lungs, and stinging eyes. Smog is also harmful to plant life.

Acid Rain

Acid rain forms when the gases sulfur dioxide and nitrogen dioxide mix with water vapor in the air. These gases form acids that fall to the earth when it rains or snows. Most of the gases that cause acid rain come from the gasoline burned by cars or from coal burned by large industries. Once they are released into the atmosphere, sulfur and nitrogen gases may travel far before they fall to earth as acid rain. Even areas that produce little pollution may receive acid rain that has traveled from other areas.

In many parts of Europe and North America, lakes and forests have been badly damaged by acid rain. In lake water the acids kill the smallest forms of life. Since these are an important source of food for all other lake animals, whole lakes may starve to death. Acid rain also "starves" forests by reducing important minerals in the soil. In both lakes and forests, poisonous metals may increase so much that they poison plant and animal life.

The Greenhouse Effect

Burning fossil fuels such as coal, oil, and gas might actually be raising our atmosphere's temperature. This is because fossil fuels all release carbon dioxide when they are burned. Carbon dioxide and water in the air form a shield around our planet. Heat waves from the sun pass through this shield to reach the earth's surface. But they cannot easily pass out again into outer space. This process keeping our planet warm is known as the greenhouse effect. Without this shield around the earth, our planet would be too cold to support life. But scientists fear that burning fossil fuels may be adding too much carbon dioxide to our atmosphere, trapping more heat than needed.

ENERGY

BALANCE
OF
NATURE

Coal—The Burning Rock

Of all the fossil fuels, coal has probably been used longer than any other. Four thousand years ago, Europeans found that these black rocks gave off more heat than burning wood. Today we still use coal in open fireplaces. But new ways of treating and burning coal have been found to release more of its stored-up heat.

The earth still holds a lot of coal. This means that as oil and gas run out, we will probably depend more and more on this solid fuel. Coal can be used in many different ways. It can be changed into a liquid or gas, burned directly, or used to make electricity.

Getting the Coal

As you've learned, coal forms underground. But not all coal lies deep beneath the planet's surface. The earth's crust is always shifting. Sometimes these movements push a layer of coal up toward the surface. This surface coal is easier to reach than the coal buried deeper. But removing it can leave scars on the landscape.

Huge earth-moving machines strip off the top layer of earth to uncover surface coal. Then cutting and digging machines remove the coal. This process is called strip mining. Strip mining can damage the land. With the soil gone, plants and trees can't grow. Where strip-mined regions are just left bare, the dry soil may simply erode (blow or wash away). To prevent this, some modern mining companies are careful to replace the topsoil after the coal has been removed. These companies plant trees and grass so the land can be as it was before.

Coal deep in the earth is more expensive and difficult to reach. Miners have to dig long shafts into the earth to allow people and equipment to get at the coal.

Deep mining is safer today than it once was. But many accidents still happen. Coal releases gases underground that can explode at the smallest spark. Layers of ground above the coal may cave in while workers are in the mine. And people breathing in coal dust for many years may develop lung diseases.

New mining methods are slowly making improvements. In the future, all underground work might be done by robotlike machines controlled by people above the surface.

Up in Smoke

Coal may be one of our most plentiful sources of energy. But it is also one of the dirtiest. Burning coal releases pollution in several forms. It produces sulfur dioxide and nitrogen oxides, both sources of acid rain. It releases carbon dioxide, which adds to the greenhouse effect. And coal releases a more poisonous form of carbon—carbon monoxide.

Yet there are cleaner ways to burn coal. Coal can be washed before burning to remove some of the solid impurities. But this does nothing to prevent coal from releasing other gases when burned. These gases can be reduced by a device called a scrubber. Scrubbers collect some of the harmful gases, such as sulfur dioxide. They trap the gases in liquid form so they don't escape into the air.

New types of coal plants actually remove harmful substances like sulfur as the coal burns. These new furnaces will make coal cleaner and produce more heat. But the new technology is very expensive. Many companies argue that the cost of adding scrubbers and new furnaces is too high. So while cleaner coal is possible, our air, water, and soil may suffer from coal pollution for many years to come. Even though coal will never provide pure, clean energy, it might have to fill the gap until we can develop cleaner energy choices.

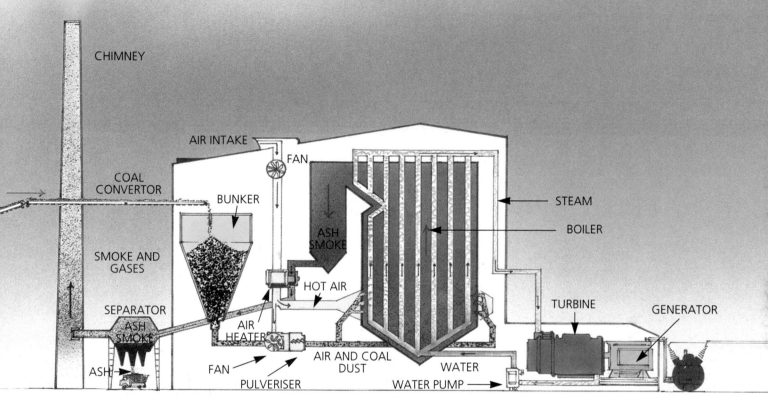

The Power of Coal

Most coal used today actually supplies us with another form of energy— electricity. Coal is burned in huge power plants that use steam to drive an electricity-making machine called a generator. The electric power made in these plants travels through supply lines to reach our homes.

The heat produced by burning coal in a furnace changes water into steam. This steam turns the large, fanlike blades of a turbine. The turbine powers a generator that produces electricity. The electricity then travels through supply lines to homes, offices, and industries where it is used.

Coal can also be turned into gas that can be carried through gas pipes for use. And someday car owners may be able to pour liquid coal into their engines instead of gasoline.

15

Filling Up With Oil and Gas

Like coal, our two most important fuels today come from beneath the earth's surface. Both oil and natural gas require expensive drilling operations to bring them to the surface. But these two fuels are so widely used that cities around the world would grind to a halt without them.

Both of these fuels can be used in many different forms. Natural gas may be brought into our homes as either a liquid or a gas. We use gas mainly for heating or for running appliances such as washing machines, dryers, and stoves. The use of natural gas to make electricity is also growing. Oil, too, is used in home heating. Oil is also processed into many different fuels, such as the gasoline used in cars, the diesel oil used in trucks, or the kerosene burned in lamps.

From Crude Oil to Fuel

The oil that comes from the ground is not the same oil we pour into furnaces or use to keep bicycle chains rust free. Oil from the ground is called crude oil. It must be improved, or refined, before it can be used. Crude oil is high in harmful sulfur. Refining removes much of the sulfur and separates crude oil into many parts. Each part is used for a different purpose.

Refining is begun by heating the crude oil. Different parts of the oil turn to gas at different temperatures. For example, gasoline turns to gas at 212 degrees Fahrenheit (100 degrees Celsius). So the gas produced at this temperature is drawn off and cooled back into liquid gasoline.

Black Gold

Oil—the tarry liquid that some call "black gold"—provides us with more than just fuel. Oil can be processed into an incredible range of products. Plastic toys and tools, eyeglasses, clothes, fertilizer, and even some types of medicine can all be made from oil.

Oil is high in energy. It gives off almost three times as much heat as burning wood. Because it is liquid, it is light, easy to pour, and takes up little space. So we depend on oil a great deal. But if we continue to use oil as much as we do now, our supply will disappear within the next century.

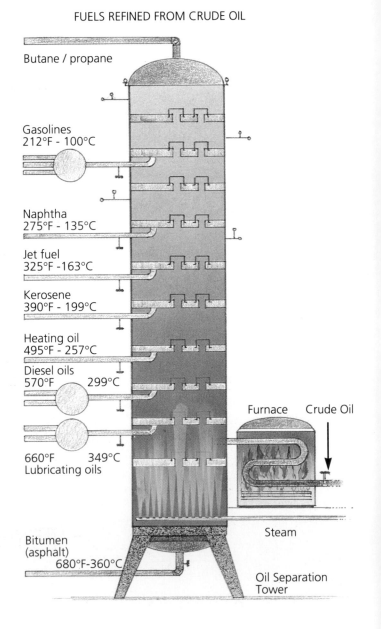

FUELS REFINED FROM CRUDE OIL

Butane / propane

Gasolines
212°F - 100°C

Naphtha
275°F - 135°C

Jet fuel
325°F -163°C

Kerosene
390°F - 199°C

Heating oil
495°F - 257°C

Diesel oils
570°F   299°C

660°F   349°C
Lubricating oils

Furnace   Crude Oil

Steam

Bitumen
(asphalt)
680°F-360°C

Oil Separation Tower

The Cost of Using Oil

Oil is found in many different parts of the world. It may be buried deep under the ocean, trapped beneath desert sands, mixed with soft layers of rock, or hidden beneath the ice near the North and South Poles. Looking for oil and removing it can damage the land and disturb wildlife. Oil tankers, for example, have often spilled their cargo at sea with deadly effects on ocean life. The refining process also produces many harmful wastes. These are buried, dumped in nearby water, or released into the air. And burning the oil breaks it down into gases that add to smog, acid rain, and the greenhouse effect.

Natural Gas—The Cleaner Cousin

Of all the fossil fuels, natural gas is the cleanest. It releases less carbon, sulfur, and nitrogen gases when it burns. Natural gas is not believed to be a major cause of acid rain. But it is still not a perfect source of energy.

Natural gas is mostly methane. Methane is one of the major causes of the greenhouse effect. It reacts in sunlight to produce carbon dioxide and water vapor, the main ingredients of the blanket around the earth that traps the sun's rays.

Methane also damages part of the earth's atmosphere called the ozone layer. The ozone layer screens out certain harmful rays from the sun. These rays, called ultraviolet radiation, can damage skin cells and growing plants.

Today natural gas provides one fifth of the energy we use. Even though it releases methane, natural gas seems to be less harmful than either oil or coal. In the near future, it may be used more and more in place of these other fossil fuels.

Natural gas

Captain Conservation: Keeping Your Cool at Home

You can cut pollution and save energy at home by turning down the heat. Just lowering the thermostat from 68 to 60 degrees Fahrenheit (20 to 15 degrees Celsius) while you are out or in bed can cut your heating bill by as much as 14 percent.

Biomass—Energy From Wood and Waste

As we begin to run out of fossil fuels, people are looking more closely at earth's never-ending power supplies. Renewable energies such as sunshine, wind, tides, biomass, and the heat from the earth's core will never run out. Many of them are also gentle on the environment because they don't release pollutants. But renewable energy sources provide less than a quarter of the energy we use today. We have only started to learn how to capture some of earth's simplest types of energy.

Biomass is the most widely used renewable energy in the world. It gives us about one sixth of our energy. But in developing areas such as parts of Africa, Asia, and South America, biomass provides half of all the energy used. In these regions people burn dried manure, wood, and other types of vegetable matter to create heat and light—even to run cars in some areas!

The Firewood Crisis

In the poorest regions scraps of wood may be the only source of fuel. As people compete for wood, many areas have been stripped clean of trees. This causes several problems. Without trees, the land may begin to erode. Tree roots act as sponges, which hold on to water in the soil. Without roots, the soil dries and is easily removed by wind or heavy rain. People also suffer from the loss of trees. Without fuel for fires, people can't cook food or heat water for cleaning.

Clearing trees also adds to global warming. Trees take in carbon dioxide to make oxygen and food. As trees disappear, carbon dioxide builds up in the air. This adds to the greenhouse effect.

Tree replanting is the best solution to the firewood crisis. But the need for wood is so great in some areas that trees cannot be planted fast enough.

It may be a dirty business, but there's money to be made in the smelly gases that build up at landfill sites. Developers are finding ready markets for the gas produced by rotting garbage. This year alone, landfill gas is expected to save British energy consumers 12 million pounds (19 million U.S. dollars). Instead of coal, the gas can be burned in boilers and furnaces. Close to twenty landfill sites are being tapped around the country, with more projects planned for the coming year.

Energy From Garbage?

Most of our garbage today is either buried in large dumping grounds called landfills or burned in special furnaces. Burning garbage releases many types of pollution into the air. Landfills take up space and produce unpleasant gases. But some countries are finding that these evil-smelling gases can be a valuable source of energy.

As buried waste breaks down, it releases gas containing carbon dioxide and methane. As these find their way into the atmosphere, both add to the greenhouse effect. Methane also attacks the ozone layer. But if these gases are collected, they can be used as fuel. In the United States, England, and Germany today, gas from some landfill sites is used to run machines that make electricity. Using this waste gas reduces the build-up of gases that changes the earth's temperature and damages the ozone layer.

Making the Best of What You Have

Just about any type of waste can be burned as fuel. So people in some energy-poor areas have been creative about using what they have for fuel. In Brazil, for example, people grow a lot of sugar cane. Today more than one quarter of the cars in Brazil run on a gas called ethanol. Ethanol is a type of alcohol made from sugar cane.

In some developing countries a substance called biogas is used as both a fuel and a fertilizer. Biogas, a mixture of methane and carbon dioxide, is made from manure and dead plant matter. To make biogas, wastes[1] are buried underground in an airtight container.[2] As the wastes break down,[3] they produce a gas[4] that can be collected and used to light stoves and lamps, or as a fuel to run machines. The leftover wastes can be plowed back into the fields as fertilizer. By the mid-1980s nearly fifty developing countries had biogas projects at work.

Gas Outlet

Biogas Chamber

Outlet Chamber

The Power of Water

If you've ever stood next to a waterfall, you know the power of rushing water. Anything caught in its path is quickly swept away. People have used the energy of moving water to do work for many years. But since the invention of the electric bulb, the greatest use of water power has been to make electricity. Electricity made by the power of moving water is called hydroelectricity, or simply hydropower. In 1895 the Niagara Falls Hydroelectric Power Station was built on the border of the United States and Canada. This began a new age of hydroelectric power. Today one quarter of all our electricity comes from hydropower.

Hydropower is usually taken from the moving waters of rivers or falls. But the power of ocean waves and tides can also be captured. Altogether the earth's water has much more energy to offer than we have been using.

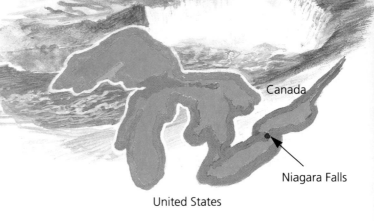

NIAGARA FALLS

Canada

Niagara Falls

United States

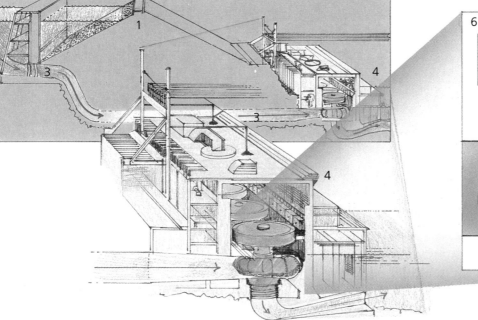

WATER TURBINE AND GENERATOR

Inside a Hydropower Station

Most hydropower stations today are built around a dam.[1] The dam traps a huge reserve of water.[2] Pipelines[3] lead the water down to a station built below the level of the dam.[4] In the station the force of the rushing water is used to turn turbines.[5] Turbines are large engines with blades like jet propellers. The power of the spinning turbines is used to turn an electricity-making machine called a generator.[6] At the heart of a generator is an electromagnetic core.[7] It is this core that actually produces the electricity. Since hydropower stations are often found in faraway, hilly regions, the electricity must travel great distances so people can use it. It is carried through wires in overhead power lines such as the ones you might spot in your own town.

Before

After

Dams are built in areas where a large reservoir can be contained. Deep valleys are filled with water, destroying their beauty as well as the wildlife habitats.

WAVE ACTION POWER GENERATOR

OFFSHORE POWER GENERATOR

The Dangers of Dams

Hydropower is cheap, nonpolluting, and renewable. But the dams that must be built can do great damage to the land. Dams usually cause flooding over a wide area. People who live in the region must move elsewhere. Plants and animals in the region lose their homes as well. Some of these plants and animals may not be able to live in other areas.

Flooding caused by dams can also spread disease because water provides an ideal place for many disease-carrying insects to breed. Dams also affect life downstream by trapping fine sand called silt. This holds back nutrients so that below the dam, water plants don't get the food they need. As plants die, so do the animals that depend on them for food. The whole balance of life in a river may be broken in this way.

Ocean Motion

Oceans may not provide the plunging force of a waterfall, but they are always on the move. Energy can be trapped from two types of ocean movement: the back-and-forth pull of the tides and the rise and fall of waves.

Tidal power is used today at just a few sites. Workers build a dam across the mouth of a bay or inlet that receives high tides. The dam allows tidal water to flow in but traps the water as it flows out. The trapped water is used to drive turbines to make electricity.

Unfortunately, tides move only twice a day. So scientists are experimenting with ways to make use of the constant motion of waves. In the future, strings of floating turbines might lace stretches of ocean. These turbines would use the rocking motion of waves to make electricity.

Heat From the Ocean

In the warm oceans south of the equator, you might someday see odd-looking power plants floating on the water. In the ocean off the coast of countries such as Indonesia, the surface water can be as warm as 80 degrees Fahrenheit (27 degrees Celsius). This warm water can be used to turn a special liquid that boils at low temperature into a gas. Just like in a steam engine, the pressure of the gas could be used to spin turbines to make electricity. Warm sea water might someday be a cheap, clean, and plentiful supply of energy for countries that need power but have little money for buying fuel.

The oceans may be a huge, untapped source of energy for the future. But we are a long way from being able to use much of this energy. We first have to develop ways to get the energy where it's needed.

21

Turning On the Sun

Whether we think about it or not, we use the heat of the sun to do a great deal of work every day. Together with the wind, the sun helps dry laundry on a clothesline, grows our food, and melts the snow. With a little more work and invention, we can trap the power from the sun to do much more for us. Each year, the sun sends as much energy to earth as 500,000 billion barrels of oil. Yet we only use a tiny fraction of this. Capturing more of the power of the sun—solar energy—is one of the greatest challenges of our energy future.

SOLAR HEATED WATER SYSTEM

Solar panels heat water as it passes through the pipes

Hot water

Cold water

Staying Warm at Home

The sun already provides heat to homes and other buildings just by shining on walls and through windows. With a few simple changes in design, homes can be built to make the best natural use of sunlight. For example, windows that face south take in the sun's rays for more hours each day. Glazed windows hold the heat inside. Special air vents can keep air moving so the whole house is kept warm. Steps like these are called "passive" solar-heating systems.

"Active" solar-heating systems use the power of the sun to heat water. Solar panels made of metal or plastic attract the sun's rays. Water passing through the panels is heated by these rays. This hot water can then be stored in tanks or used right away for heating or washing. A series of pipes carries the water throughout the building.

Not all parts of the world get enough sunlight to make good use of solar energy. In many homes in these areas, solar energy can begin the heating process. But oil, gas, or electricity must be used in furnaces to supply extra heat. Starting with solar energy at least cuts down on the amount of fossil fuel needed in these homes.

Sunshine Into Steam

The power of the sun can be used for much more than direct heating. Even in areas where the sun doesn't shine every day, its power can be used to make steam to drive electricity-making turbines.

You probably know that passing sunlight through a magnifying glass increases its strength. The sun's rays can be made so hot that they start fires. This principle is used at the giant "solar furnace" at Odeillo, France. There a curved wall made of thousands of mirrors concentrates the power of the sun. Temperatures in this "solar furnace" can reach over 6000 degrees Fahrenheit (3300 degrees Celsius). The heat is used to make steam, which drives turbines to make electricity.

Solar Cells

Sunshine can also be turned into electricity with the technology of solar cells. Solar cells are made of a layer of metal coated in special substances. These substances produce a flow of electricity when struck by sunlight. You may have seen watches or calculators that seem to run magically on sunshine. This is made possible by solar cells.

In order to make a lot of electricity, a great number of solar cells are needed. In the past, the high cost of preparing a material called silicon for use in solar cells made them too expensive for large projects. But as technology improves, solar cells are dropping in price. Someday electricity made from the sun may be cheaper than that made by coal-, hydro-, or gas-powered plants.

A Sunny Future?

Of all the forms of renewable energy, sunshine may be our greatest hope. But a lot of research must be done before large solar projects become practical. In the meantime, solar power is best used in small projects, especially in areas that get a lot of sunshine. Since 1982 three villages in the desert of Saudi Arabia have received their energy from a solar power plant. In 1983 the United States built its first solar power plant in southern California. These first solar power plants were small, but they have already led the way for larger plants in many regions.

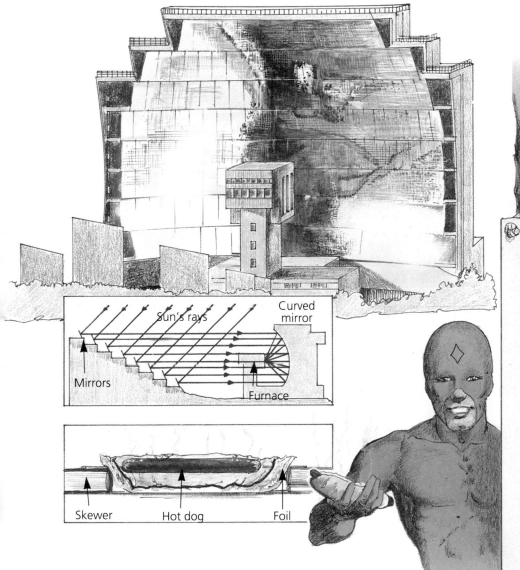

Sun's rays — Curved mirror — Mirrors — Furnace

Skewer — Hot dog — Foil

Captain Conservation: Try a Solar-Heated Hot Dog!

On a sunny day you can use the power of the sun to cook a hot dog. Use a piece of tinfoil that measures about twelve inches by twelve inches (thirty and a half centimeters by thirty and a half centimeters). Curve the sides of your foil so that it forms a shallow bowl. Place a hot dog on a skewer so that it rests about halfway up from the bottom of the foil bowl. Rest both ends of the skewer on a stack of books or other objects to hold the hot dog in place. Leave the solar heater in the sun, turning the hot dog from time to time. In fifteen minutes to half an hour, your hot dog should be cooked and ready to eat. Test it first by breaking off an end to be sure the inside is done.

Traditional (Dutch)   Modern (French)

ILLUSTRATION IS TO SCALE

AMERICAN FOOTBALL FIELD

THE PROPELLERS OF A MODERN WIND
MACHINE CAN BE AS LONG AS A
FOOTBALL FIELD

Capturing the Wind

The power of wind can range from gentle breezes to fierce hurricanes. Using this power is nothing new. For thousands of years, sailors have used wind power to carry their boats across water. Farmers have used windmills to grind grain and pump water for centuries. In the twentieth century our knowledge of airplane propellers has helped us produce more powerful wind machines. These machines use the power of wind to make electricity.

Eggbeater or Propeller

Modern wind machines use huge blades to capture the wind. The blades spin in the wind, sending their power down a central pole to a turbine. The turbine drives a generator to make electricity.

Most wind machines look much like the propellers of an airplane. They have two long blades that spin when facing the wind. A wind machine designed in France looks more like a whisk or an eggbeater. Two curved blades form an arc along either side of the central pole. This model will spin in wind from any direction.

Powerful Eyesores?

Wind power may be clean and plentiful. But in order to make large quantities of electricity, many wind turbines have to be used together. Since they are only useful in a windy area, turbines are placed together in towering rows. Not everyone likes to have these giant turbines in their area. The view of the surrounding landscape can be ruined by hundreds of wind machines, eighty feet (twenty-four meters) tall.

In the future, wind turbines might be built off the coast. There they can capture strong ocean winds and be less of an eyesore. Of course, boat traffic might not be happy with these towering intruders in the water!

Surface

3 Miles
4.8 Km.

6 Miles
9.6 Km.

9 Miles
14.5 Km.

Bore hole

Magma

Earth's Underground Furnace

From time to time, volcanoes erupt on the earth's surface, sending hot lava and ash spewing up from below the ground. These volcanoes are a reminder that the earth itself is like a huge furnace. It is cool at the surface but hot enough to melt lead at its core.

In the growing search for clean energy, we are beginning to look underground to see how much we can use of earth's heat. For the most part this heat, called geothermal energy, is captured in the form of steam.

Tapping Hot Springs

Besides its reserves of gas, oil, and coal, the earth's crust holds underground pockets of water. Heat from the earth's core keeps this water hot.

In some areas cracks in the earth's surface allow some of this hot water to escape as steam. At The Geysers, 90 miles (145 kilometers) north of San Francisco, California, the world's largest geothermal plant captures this steam. The pressure from the steam is used to run turbines to make electricity. By the mid-1980s The Geysers were producing enough electricity for a city of one million people.

But not all regions are lucky enough to have steam escape directly from the ground. Some underground water reserves are not hot enough to make steam. But their heat can be used to change other liquids to gas. Some liquids boil at a lower temperature than water. The gas produced by these liquids can be used to drive turbines in the same way that steam can.

Drilling for Magma

Deep below the earth's surface, the temperature is so high that rock is in liquid form. The liquid rock is called magma. In 1989 American scientists began drilling deep into the earth. Their goal was to see if magma could be used to heat water sent down from the earth's surface. To reach the magma, a hole must be dug four to six miles (six and a half to nine and a half kilometers) into the earth. If the experiments are successful, power plants in the twenty-first century might run on steam made from the heat of magma. Water would be pumped downward through a pipe. Once it reached the hot magma, the water would turn to steam. The steam would then return to the surface through a smaller protected pipe.

The Mighty Atom

Energy is not just found in moving wind or water or in the fuels we burn. Energy is also locked up in the smallest units that make up all matter in the universe. These units of matter are called atoms. Atoms are held together by powerful bonds. It was the famous scientist Albert Einstein who first suggested that splitting the atom by breaking these bonds would release a great amount of energy.

Splitting an atom is no easy matter. The bonds that hold an atom together are very strong. Atoms are made up of a central core called a nucleus and particles called electrons that circle around the nucleus. The nucleus is made up of particles called protons and neutrons. Different substances have different numbers of protons and neutrons in the nuclei of their atoms. Only those with overcrowded nuclei are useful for releasing energy because they are more easily split.

When the nucleus of an overcrowded atom is hit by a free neutron (a neutron not contained within a nucleus), the atom splits. If enough of these overcrowded atoms are present, a chain reaction takes place as other stray neutrons hit more atoms.

A great amount of energy in the form of heat is released as the atoms split apart. If not controlled, this energy can produce a powerful explosion. But when other materials are used to slow and contain the reaction, the energy can be used as a source of power.

For War or Peace?

In August 1945 the cities of Hiroshima and Nagasaki in Japan were destroyed by the most powerful bombs the world had ever seen up to that time. Hundreds of thousands of people died instantly. Thousands more have suffered from the effects of the bombing since then.

From this terrible beginning the use of nuclear energy—the power of the atom—has switched to more peaceful purposes. Beginning in the 1950s, power plants were built to supply electricity made from nuclear energy. Early energy planners had high hopes for the future of nuclear energy. They predicted that by the year 2000 half of the world's electricity would come from nuclear power.

But by the early 1990s only about one sixth of the world's electric supply was coming from nuclear energy. And around the world, angry citizens protested the opening of new plants. What went wrong with plans for the peaceful use of nuclear energy? Part of the answer lies in the deadly wastes produced by nuclear power.

No Place for Waste

As atoms split in a nuclear reaction, they produce substances that release dangerous particles. These invisible particles can pass through skin cells, damaging the body in many different ways. These substances are said to be radioactive.

Most nuclear reactors use rods or pellets of a fuel called uranium. The fuel rods are only good for a few years. After use, these rods are full of radioactive substances released when the uranium atoms split. So they have to be handled carefully. Once they have cooled, the wastes are encased in steel and coated in concrete. They are then buried underground in concrete containers.

Some of these wastes stay radioactive for thousands, even millions of years. No one has yet found a safe way to store these wastes for that long. Some people suggest burying them far under the earth or ocean. But we can't be completely sure that movements in the earth's crust won't disturb them sometime in the future. These wastes may be a troublesome gift to our great-great-grandchildren.

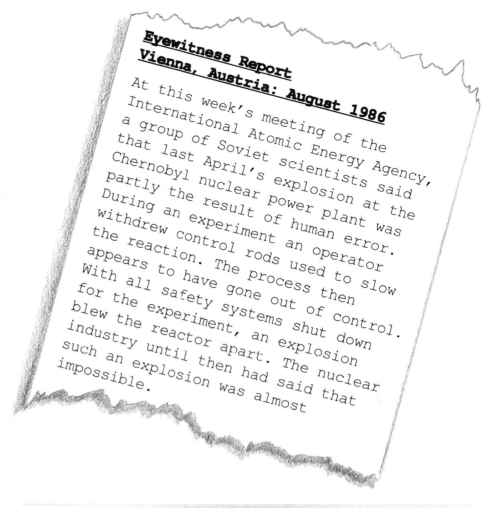

Eyewitness Report
Vienna, Austria: August 1986

At this week's meeting of the International Atomic Energy Agency, a group of Soviet scientists said that last April's explosion at the Chernobyl nuclear power plant was partly the result of human error. During an experiment an operator withdrew control rods used to slow the reaction. The process then appears to have gone out of control. With all safety systems shut down for the experiment, an explosion blew the reactor apart. The nuclear industry until then had said that such an explosion was almost impossible.

Cleaner, Safer Reactors?

In the past, a number of reactors in which nuclear energy is produced have been the sites of accidents. This has made nuclear power expensive and has caused people to worry about its safety. But new designs for nuclear reactors may make this a safer, cleaner, and cheaper source of energy in the future.

Older power plants depended on workers and many levels of safety systems to prevent accidents. New designs rely on natural forces such as gravity and expanding gas to cool reactors. These new, simpler safety controls that depend less on people to prevent accidents are called "passive" features. The new reactors will also be smaller and use less fuel. This will make them less expensive and less likely to have a large accident.

With these changes, nuclear energy may have a second chance. It may solve some of our energy needs by providing cheap electricity without the pollution of coal or oil. But until we find a way to store nuclear waste safely, we may be saving today's environment at the expense of tomorrow's.

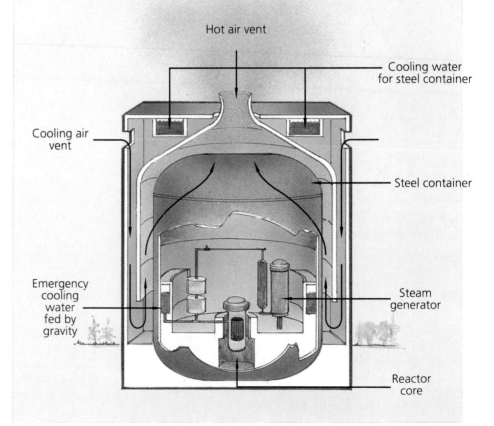

Hot air vent

Cooling water for steel container

Cooling air vent

Steel container

Emergency cooling water fed by gravity

Steam generator

Reactor core

An Energy-Wise Future

We have learned over the years that all energy has a cost. We pay for energy with the money spent on utility bills. But we also pay for it with our air, water, and soil. If we don't choose and use energy wisely, it may cost us a safe and livable planet.

Acid rain, the greenhouse effect, smog, and damage to the ozone layer have shown us the dangers of burning fossil fuels. But even if we wanted to stop using these fuels tomorrow, we probably could not. Safer, cleaner energy sources such as the sun, wind, and tide are still many years away from supplying our needs. Nuclear power is still not safe and affordable.

We don't have one magic source that can supply all our energy cheaply and cleanly. But we can reduce the harm done by many fuels by using them wisely. Here are some ways in which our fuels can be made to last longer and do less damage.

Turning Off the Power

The best way to use energy is to use it as little as possible! During the 1970s an oil shortage forced people to use energy more wisely. Even though their industries were growing, many countries used far less energy. This proved that we can get by with less fuel. But when there doesn't seem to be a shortage, we use more energy than we need.

Many devices can help us save energy. Some types of cars run on less fuel than others. Homes that are well insulated need less energy for heating and cooling. Washing machines and showers can be fitted with devices that use less hot water. People can save a great deal of energy by using these devices and simply by remembering to turn lights and machines off when they are not needed.

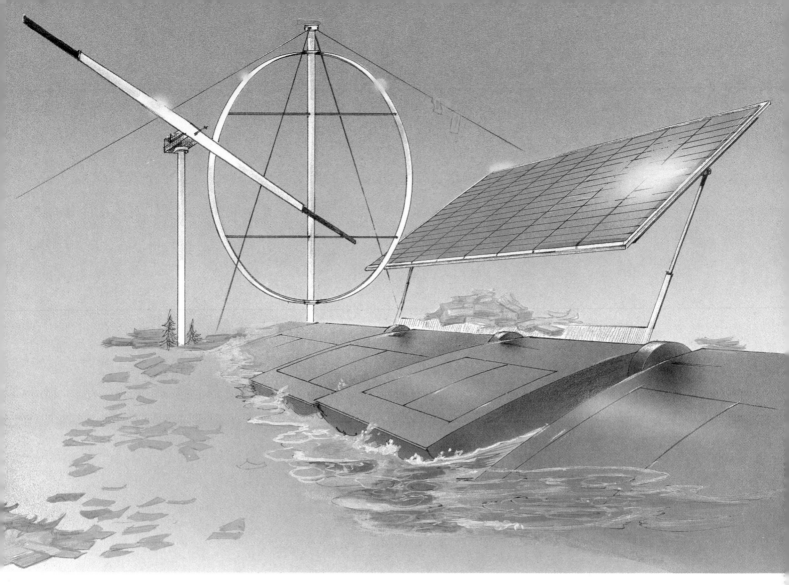

Cleaner Smokestacks and Exhaust Pipes

We can't switch from fossil fuels right away, but we can at least clean the wastes these fuels send into the air. Scrubbers can be added to factories to collect many of the polluting gases that would normally go up their smokestacks. Cars can be fitted with devices called catalytic converters. These devices change a car's acid-making nitrogen oxides into harmless nitrogen.

Cleaning devices such as scrubbers and catalytic converters don't remove all harmful gases produced by fossil fuels. But they help us cut back on some of the worst polluters.

Using Energy From Around Us

Until cheaper and more practical ways are found to take large amounts of power from the sun, wind, and tide, these sources can't meet all our needs. But they do make a lot of sense in many regions. Solar power might not be practical for foggy London, England. But it can supply a great deal of energy to sunny places like southern California or northern Africa. Wind and tide won't supply power to everyone either. But they can be captured and used in many coastal areas around the world.

By using renewable energy in small, local projects, we can cut down on the total amount of fossil fuels we need.

Saving Fossil Fuels for Special Jobs

Many of the jobs we use energy for offer us a choice. For example, most homes can be heated with oil, gas, or electricity. For other jobs, we might only have one choice of fuel. For instance, most cars will only run on some form of gasoline. We can begin to save fossil fuels by using them only when there is no other practical choice.

Investing in the Future

Developing new sources of energy takes a lot of time and money. Billions of dollars are spent finding and opening up new oil fields. More billions have been spent on building nuclear power plants. This is all money that has been invested in our energy future.

By comparison, very little money has been spent on developing solar, tidal, or wind power. We won't be able to use these energy sources widely until more research is done on them. This may mean changing the way we spend money on energy.

Doing Our Part for Tomorrow's Energy

No one person will be able to find the solution to our energy problems. Saving the energy we have and using cleaner fuels are something we must all take part in. As you grow older, you will make many decisions about energy use. You may choose to buy a car that burns gasoline. You might own a home someday and have to choose a practical way to heat it. You will choose between many different tools and appliances that all must run on some type of energy.

But even today you can start to think about how to use energy more wisely. Each day, you probably use energy in hundreds of different ways. On the following page are a few things you can start doing right away to cut down and clean up your energy use.

✔ Don't waste hot water. It takes energy to heat water. When you waste it, you are pouring expensive energy down the drain.

✔ Remember to turn off lights, stereo, television, and any other appliances when you are finished using them. The electricity these use may well come from a power plant that runs on coal or nuclear power. The less you use, the less pollution these plants will produce.

✔ Try to cut down on the amount of time you spend using devices that need energy. Instead of watching television, why not have fun by flying a kite, drawing pictures, playing ball, or reading a book outdoors or in a sunlit area? These activities don't burn fuel, and they'll keep your mind and body strong!

✔ Don't waste the things you own. All of the products we buy in stores—clothes, records, toys, and much more—take a great deal of energy to make. As you throw these things away and replace them with new products, more energy is used.

Index